DRAGON RIDER

CONNOR WHITELEY

No part of this book may be reproduced in any form or by any electronic or mechanical means. Including information storage, and retrieval systems, without written permission from the author except for the use of brief quotations in a book review.

This book is NOT legal, professional, medical, financial or any type of official advice.

Any questions about the book, rights licensing, or to contact the author, please email connorwhiteley@connorwhiteley.net

Copyright © 2022 CONNOR WHITELEY

All rights reserved.

DEDICATION
Thank you to all my readers without you I couldn't do what I love.

DRAGON RIDER

Feeling the cold bitter wind brush past his smooth skin, Cato felt a small shiver run down his spine. As the wind continued to blow constantly, he could feel his skin become dry and harsh. But that was life out here.

In a corner of the Realm where problems that needed to go where sent. To a normal man that fact would make them rageful but not Cato.

With the cold wind continuing to brush his skin, Cato kept looking out over the immense cliff edge. Smiling as he looked out over the thousands of kilometres of lust green forests, farmlands and rivers.

He supposed this was a perk of his banishment. At least Cato could wake up to this stunning view each morning. There was just something magical about how the immense thick green trees blow in the wind and the river swirled and twirled that made Cato have a moment of peace. Just for the briefest of times. As Cato moved his feet, he felt the smooth rock beneath him crack a little from the movement.

Deciding his time of looking aimlessly over the cliff was over, Cato turned around, feeling the rock under his feet chip as he turned.

He smiled as he looked back at his home in these harsh mountains. Before Cato was banished or exiled here, he never would have understood how people would love the cold, damp mountains. But after being here for five years, he could understand it now.

Cato rolled his eyes as he saw a broken slate tile on the floor instead of being on his little stone hut about a hundred metres away. Something else he would have to fix later on.

The howling of the wind calmed a little. Allowing Cato to hear the laughter and talking of young men and women on the other side of the little outpost or home. He had no idea what this place was actually called.

Turning his head ever so slightly to the left, Cato smiled a little to see the men and women waking up and coming out of their own little small stone huts with their thatch roofs. Then he cocked his head at the sight of all of their chimneys puffing out smoke. They must have gotten up early to have a raging fire already going.

At least he wouldn't have to do a wake up call like he did a few times a week. That was a positive. Cato hated wake up calls with a passion. He might have been the Lord Dragon Rider, in charge of these trainees, but to have to wake them up? Really?

Shaking the thoughts away, Cato turned around once again to look out on the stunning view. Then he realised why the trainees were awake so early. They probably wanted to see the new person as soon as they arrived.

King Only Knows why this newbie wanted to arrive at the crack of dawn instead of a normal time. Granted Cato was usually awake at this time already but he would rather clean out the Dragonlets styles. Or talk to his own dragon then wait around for some newbie. And why would the trainees be so interested?

It's not like they don't see new people here often. They had ten new girls join last week to replace the twenty Dragon Riders that departed to go off with their dragons to some far away battle.

The thought of battle made Cato touch his forehead as the large scar across his forehead and face pulsed with pain. That was a battle and half alright. Cato smiled as the lust for battle flooded his body. Yet it died quickly as his mind became flooded with the faces of his dead friends and soldiers.

The sound of claws hitting rock caught Cato's attention. Making him turn around and beam with delight as he saw an immense, majestic dragon with stunning shiny blue scales land. Her head majestically rose in the air and stretched before she lowered it down to Cato's level.

He stroked his beautiful dragon's stout as she smiled. Showing all her mighty yet terrifying rows of sharp dagger like teeth. Cato definitely loved this dragon. He knew that for sure.

"Morning Catty," the stunning dragon started to speak in a voice that did not match her majestic nature in the slightest.

"Morning Pendra,"

"Why ya trainees up earlier, gov?"

"I think I should be asking you that. What did you tell them about our new arrival?"

"You know me. Ma lips are tight and sealed. I don't tell them a thing,"

"What did you tell the other dragons and dragonlets?"

Pendra tried to rub her snout into Cato's warm stomach but Cato pushed her away.

"What did you tell them?"

"I could have told them that ya newbie is gay, exiled and a Former Commander"

Cato had to smile and run his fingers over Pendra's smooth shiny snout.

"They wanted to know if me and the newbie would hit it off?"

"They are ya words, not mine"

Cato did have to cock his head for a moment at the thought of meeting another gay person after years of being isolated and stuck teaching young people about how to become Dragon Riders.

But really did everyone need to come out to see this, everyone knew Cato was gay. It was the reason he was exiled and sent to this place. Not the worse place because Cato did have an uncanny ability to match and train dragons and humans. But that couldn't be the only reason.

Cato straightened his head to look at Pendra again. The dragon gave an elegant yet scary smile as her dagger like teeth came out of her mouth. Then the other reason came to mind.

"Former Commander you said?"

"Ya Catty. One of the Five. One was of the Five legendary warriors. He was outed and exiled. Sent here ya know. Stripped of ranked and all,"

Cato kissed Pendra's stout and started to walk towards to the trainees' huts a few hundred metres away. He had to admit it was weird that a Commander had been sent here. Even a gay one. Something wasn't right.

After a few seconds of walking, Cato stopped and turned around to face Pendra.

"Pendra my dear, I have a job for you. A job only you're good enough for,"

"What ya want Catty?"

"I need you to go to the Lord Commander and find out why whoever his Commander is, got stripped of his rank and title?"

"Thought that was obvious. He's a gay exile. Don't ya all get stripped of titles and sent here,"

"Not exactly. Most gay people in the Realm get treated the same as everyone else. But if you're in a position of power then you get exiled by your enemies. But you don't get your titles stripped for being gay. I still have mine,"

"That is true. Still don't know why ya don't use your titles,"

"You know why. Can you go to the Lord Commander please? I know he's fighting orks on the other side of the Realm. But you're the fastest dragon in the Realm,"

Pendra rose her shiny blue head high up as she presumably thought about it.

"Only on one condition. We go for a long ride. Just us two. Like we did in ya Rider days,"

"I would like nothing more," Cato smiled.

"Then make sure ya don't get into any trouble without me,"

Cato nodded and Pendra gave him a quick kiss, Cato almost jumped at the touch of her cold smooth scales, before she flew off into the distance.

He had to admire her stunning scaly wings as they flexed and move with such elegance with the howling wind as she raced off to the other side of the Realm.

Cato knew some people would call it foolish for him to send his dragon off for something so petty. But Cato knew the Lord Commander would appreciate having Pendra there and fighting even if it was only for a few hours.

Another loud sound of claws hitting rock came from behind. Turning around Cato would feel his eyes widen and a massive smile starting to form on his face but he had to quickly stop his face as he looked upon the stunning newbie.

The Lord Dragonrider wanted to kick himself at these thoughts. He was a man in his late twenties in charge of training new Dragon Riders for the King. Not some horny common person. But he had to admit the newbie was amazing.

Pretending to be sizing him up, Cato looked him up then shrugged. He wasn't going to let the newbie know he found him attractive. Cato was too well versed in political battles for him to do that.

Granted he did admire the newbie's tall muscular frame with his sharp, handsome face with his attractive longish blond hair parted to the right.

A part of Cato wanted to walk up to the newbie and run his fingers through it. But Cato really wanted to kick himself at the thought. This was not the time!

Although, his eyes narrowed as Cato realised this Former Commander had also been stripped of his armour. Instead the newbie just wore a tight white tunic and some leather trousers. Of course, per Dragon Rider protocol, Cato would have to give him some armour, but he could always delay that by a few hours. Given how tight the newbie's tunic was.

He smiled a little at the thought of finding out what this person did. Given how dishonourable it is to have your armour stripped in addition to your titles and rank.

Pulling his attention away from the newbie, Cato beamed and gave a boyish laugh as he saw the newbie's dragon.

Just looking at the Dragon's immense muscular frame and powerful wings was amazing. And the way the morning sun sparkled off his fiery orange scales was impressive. In return, the dragon bowed his head elegantly.

Cato's smile deepened the respect the dragon had shown. It was rare for a Commander's dragon to show respect to a 'lesser'. Maybe this was a good addition to the mountain.

Although, it was odd that the dragon smelt of sweet oranges and the stunning newbie smelt of some kind of earthy aftershave. Had they really prepared themselves for their arrival?

In an attempt to show the newbie he was in charge here, Cato simply said: "And you are?"

The Lord Dragon Rider gave a crooked smile when he saw the newbies face turned to confusion and gave him a strange look. This was definitely going to be fun.

After a few seconds, his beautiful dragon gave him a gentle poke in the ribs.

"Oh yes, I am Commander Caden of the Royal Guard, Slayer of the Dark Ork, Liberator of..."

"You are no Commander anymore. You are a man stripped of armour and rank. Even if you had these things in *my* training facility. They would mean little,"

Cato smiled at Caden as the former commander's face turned pale and shock. His mouth even dropped a little. Clearly he had never been spoken to in this way before. But Cato wasn't going to let some arrogant fool into his training facility. No matter how attractive he was.

"I am still a Commander. I am a Hero with hundreds of names detailing my honours. I am the best fighter…"

Cato completely ignored him and walked up to his stunning orange dragon. He breathed in a little more as the dragon's smell of sweet oranges filled his senses. Reminding him of his time as a child playing under the orange trees with his sister.

"And who is this fine dragon? Just look at him. Strong bones, strong wings. Must be one of the last dragons from the far North. I am sorry for your lost Dragon. Those wars never should have happened,"

Cato could feel Caden wanting to speak but his dragon stared at him. Caden turned quiet. Before his dragon bowed in respect at Cato once more.

"The Lord Commander did not tell me this human was so softly spoken. He is a flatterer yet honest. Um, I think this new home will be good for us. I am Kadien," the dragon boomed in a strong fear provoking voice.

Cato gave the dragon a quick bow in return.

"It is an honour to meet you too, Kadien. I am Lord Dragon Rider Cato," he turned to see Caden's amazing crystal blue eyes stare at him. " And I too have hundreds of names, but I do not boast about them,"

"Do not mind him, Human. He is not use to being around other people that outrank him. I will do my best to keep him in line,"

"Thank you," Cato returned.

The sound of footsteps made Cato look at the stone huts as he saw a tall slim boy walking towards them. He knew it was one of the trainees but this wasn't the most spoken of the trainees. They all must have drawn straws or stones to pick who would come over here. And that made Cato smile a little.

"My Lord," the boy said nervously as he looked at the terrifying dragon that could easily kill him within seconds.

"Speak,"

"My Lord, one of the Dragonlets reported sensing a dragon in distress near Angel's Fall. Should I tell the others to prepare?"

Cato paused for a moment. He always loved the ability of the young dragons to sense out members of their own kind. But a dragon was in danger. He needed to save it or find out what happened. Yet he couldn't just leave the training facility unattended. Well, not officially.

However, Cato would not let Caden remain here alone after he just turned up. Then he realised this might be what he needed. A chance to get to know Caden and his dragon. He knew he would get a visit from one of the Lord Commander's Agents in the next few weeks demanding a progress report. And who was he to let the Lord Commander down?

"Negative. I will go with *Former* Commander Caden and his fine dragon to rescue the dragon. As always, no flying whilst I'm gone and prepare me a Dragonlet,"

"Nonsense, you must fly with me and Kadien,"

Cato gestured at the boy to leave when he saw the boy smile inappropriately at Caden's offer. At least he'll have something to report to the others about.

"Caden, I can't fly with you,"

"Why not?"

Cato tried for a few seconds to think of a reason but he failed. The real reason he didn't want to go flying was because that would require Cato to wrap his arms around Caden's rather stunning body. He wanted to, he wouldn't do it. That was inappropriate. But there was a dragon that needed saving so... Cato supposed it didn't matter too much.

"Fine then. Let's go,"

Kadien started to kneel down for the two men to climb on her small brown leather saddle where Caden stopped and asked: "Where's your dragon, *my Lord?*"

"Traveling to the South Ocean to get some fish for the cook," he lied.

***

After two long hours of flying, Cato felt the wind slow as Kadien flapped his mighty orange wings a final time. Before the stunning dragon landed softly.

As Cato slipped off the hard dragon scale, he ribbed his back as the harsh feeling of dragon scales irritated his skin. And that reminded him of another reason why he didn't ride with other people.

Stretching his muscles, Cato looked around to see the kilometre high sloops of the hills around them that formed an impressive deep dip in the land. A part of Cato would have preferred if they had landed somewhere else here. Especially since being in such a deep dip in the land prevented them from seeing if a threat was approaching.

Pushing those thoughts aside, Cato started to walk away from Kaiden. Feeling the soft plants crushed under his leather booted feet as he moved. He did have to appreciate the natural beauty of the land with everything being covered in a thick layer of greenery. With sweet-smelling flowers, that left the taste of sugar on the mouth were littered around.

Then in the background, Cato heard the relaxing sound of the waterfall a few hundred metres away.

He smiled as a memory came into his mind about playing in the water under the Angel Fall with his sister as a child. They played for hours. Just two siblings without a care in the world. How times change.

Then a more interesting memory came up as he remembered the fun time him and his school friends had had jumping off the waterfall. Not a wise decision by a long stretch, but those were fun times. Definitely something Cato wouldn't be doing again though.

Turning his attention back to the task at hand, Cato's eyes narrowed as he realised there wasn't an injured dragon here. There was only him, Kaiden and the beautiful Caden.

Again, the Lord Dragon Rider rolled his eyes at himself for thinking like this on a mission. But he couldn't deny those two hours weren't pleasant. Considering he was sitting on the rough scales of a dragon's back for two hours. Even now, his legs still felt as if someone had rubbed sandpaper between them. Yet holding onto Caden's body and abs for two hours was hardly torture.

This time Cato actually kicked himself for thinking like this. He had been around attractive men all his life. So, why was this one so different?

"Are you okay, *my Lord?*"

Cato turned to face Caden who was taking his two long swords out of a small black sack on Kadien's back. The smooth and elegant motion only enhanced Caden's beauty. Then Cato remembered the question.

"Um, yes. I am fine. Just curiosity," he turned to Kadien who was stretching his impressive neck. "Are you sure this is where you sensed the dragon?"

"Are you questioning me, my Lord?"

"Of course not,"

"I don't understand Dragons and their sensing. In my army, we just focused on fighting,"

"Well, Kadien we are no longer in the army. We serve Lord Cato now,"

Cato cocked his head slightly at the harshness of the words. Clearly, the dragon wasn't impressed at his Master. Cato really wanted Pendra to come back with the information he needed.

"So, you can just sense the presence of another dragon?"

"Of course, my Lord Dragon Rider. I am a very powerful dragon. I can sense any dragon,"

Cato gestured around the dip in the land.

"Clearly, there is something wrong with my dragon abilities,"

Cato always loved dragons getting defensive. He took a few steps back and felt his leather boots sink into the ground slightly. Looking down at them for a moment, he realised they were covered in dark rich red blood.

"Kadien… if a dragon was killed. Would you be able to track that? And could *the life signal* remain detectable for a few hours?"

Cato thought the dragon was about to say something defensive about his and his Master's immense skill. Instead the poor dragon's massive eyes lit up as he realised what Cato was saying.

Caden threw Cato his weapon.

Cato caught the large double-bladed staff with ease.

He turned around. Waiting for something to happen.

There was no dragon. Not anymore.

Why would something kill a dragon?

They were protected creatures. Harming them is punishable by death.

Over the edge of the dip came a loud sound akin to screaming or chanting.

Cato tensed.

His eyes widened as he saw hundreds if not thousands of brown humanoid figures pour over the edge. Charging towards them.

Cato didn't know how the Orks had got here. But this was far from good.

Kaiden reflexed his neck high and gave an immense, deafening roar.

Cato whipped out a bone horn from his waist. He blew it as loud as he could.

Hopefully, some dragon would hear it and send help.

The brown tide of orks kept coming.

Cato broke into a fighting stance.

The orks came at him.

Cato slashed and lashed his staff.

It cut deep into their disgusting flesh.

Oily black blood splashed over his face.

Orks laid dead at his feet.

More kept coming.

Cato slashed the throats of more orks. They fell to the ground.

Stupid orks behind them fell over their former friends.

Cato didn't hesitate.

He slammed his bladed staff down on their heads.

The whipping of air made Cato dive out the way. A rusty ork sword whipped past him.

Cato slashed the throat of that ork.

Immense heat rushed past his skin. Warming it slightly.

Kadien unleashed a storm of fire at the orks. Whilst he whipped and lashed his powerful tail at the orks on the other side.

They were surrounded.

Cato kept fighting.

His arms were a constant dance of elegant moves as his staff slashed, dashed and lashed at the incoming orks.

A wall of bodies started to form around them.

It didn't take long for the orks to start using their dead friends as a platform.

Cato swung his staff high to hit them.

He screamed in rage at these horrors. How dare they come this far into his Realm.

Cato paused a moment as he saw Caden charge up and jump over the dead orks.

The Lord Dragon Rider awed as Caden elegantly and beautifully sliced through the orks. It was a stunning dance you would pay good money to see.

An ork jumped down on top of Cato.

The ork smelled disgusting of rotten meat.

Cato headbutted the ork. Before choking him to death with his staff.

Another ork grabbed him.

Cato spun around. Forcing his staff through the ork's armour.

Kadien roared in pain as several orks stabbed him.

The dragon whipped his tail around without a care.

Cato jumped to the floor as the tail almost shattered his body.

Orks screamed as their bones and muscles were shattered.

The wall of dead orks flew into the distance.

Cato couldn't see Caden.

He wanted to look for him.

He couldn't lose him.

But Cato needed to focus on the mission and surviving.

He looked up to the edge of the dip. Cato snarled a little as he saw more and more orks charging down at them.

Kadien roared once more as he let out a devastating torrent of pure fiery power at the orks.

The smell of cooked flesh filled the air.

Kadien screamed in agony.

Cato looked around.

New larger orks ran at the dragon. Holding black bottles of blue sparkling powder.

The orks threw the bottles at him.

They exploded when they smashed on the

dragon's body.

Litres of dark rich dragon blood poured onto the ground.

Cato was not having a dragon die on his watch.

He rushed over to the orks.

An immense brutish ork taggled him to the ground.

Cato felt the cold blood of the last dragon coat his skin.

The large brown disgusting ork punched her meaty fists into his head.

Cato's vision blurred.

The ork screamed at Cato. A sword shot out of its mouth.

Cato pushed the ork off from him.

Caden grabbed Cato's soft hand and pulled him up.

Cato wanted this moment to last a little longer.

Two black bottles threw their way.

Caden threw Cato to the ground. As the bottles hit him.

They exploded.

Caden screamed in agony as his tunic burned and his skin crisped.

Cato looked at the three orks holding the bottles.

He screamed at them.

The orks stopped for a moment.

Cato charged over. Jumped into the air and beheaded them.

An ear-splitting trumpet sound came from the top of the dip.

Cato wanted to sink to his knees when he saw more orks holding black bottles march towards him.

Kadien screamed once more as more bottles

exploded and battered his body.

Cato rushed over to kill more orks, but it was too late. Kadien collapsed with an immense thud as the explosions had taken their toll on him.

The Lord Dragon Rider looked into the dragon's pain filled eyes and blew the stunning creature a kiss of respect.

Turning around Cato saw the orks walk up to him. Their brown disgusting faces smiled at him as if they had won. A part of Cato thought they had.

If he was religious, then Cato would have asked for only one thing in that moment. He would have given anything to make sure Caden lived. He would have happily died as long as Caden was safe.

The rest of the orks stopped and Cato knew they covered the entire dip by now. Then a large smelly ork, that made Cato want to gag, walked up to him. Pointing a blade at his throat. This ork didn't need to say anything but he wanted to.

A torrent of blue fire shot down from the sky.

The orks screamed in agony as they burnt alive.

More torrents shot down.

Cato moved his staff. Slicing deep into the large Ork's chest.

The orks ran in fear.

Cato went to charge forward but he stopped as he saw tens of strong powerful torrents of fire rain down from the sky.

The constant storm of fire dried his skin and Cato felt sweat drip down his back and chest.

After a few minutes, all the orks were dead. There was nothing in the deep dip except Cato, Caden and Kadien. And thousands of smouldering corpses of dead orks.

A loud thud came from behind as someone spoke:

"Ya called Catty!"

***

Standing in front of a roaring crackling fire looking over the mountainous valley below, Cato felt the fire warm his front. While the freezing mountain air chilled his back.

The flames danced and swirled in the fire. Making all sorts of crazy, chaotic shadows on the mountain rock that was warmed by the fire. And oddly the rock heated Cato's feet nicely.

At least the crackling sound of the fire with the mountain wind howling in the background was better than the screaming of Kadien and beautiful Caden. And the bitter smoke smelt hundreds of times better than those disgraceful orks.

Looking deep into the flames, Cato's concern only grew about the ork threat. Of course, he had sent word to the Capital and the Lord Commander about this development. He doubted he would ever hear anything. For he was *only* a Lord Dragon Rider. But at least he had done something.

However, it wasn't the presence of orks that bothered Cato. It was the number. Thousands of orks somehow made it here. Their homelands were on the other side of the Realm. Not here.

Shaking those thoughts away for another day, Cato smiled as he thought about Caden. It was a miracle that Pendra and the other Dragon Riders from the Training Facility had found them.

Then Cato nodded his head as he remembered hearing from the trainees were less than pleased about coming out to rescue him. The only reason they were saved apparently was because one girl took charge and ordered the others to help.

Cato shook his head as he considered promoting her to something. But again though that was a thought for another day. This day had been too long for comfort.

The gentle sound of claws hitting rock made Cato lean back. As he sensed Pendra curl around the fire. Leaning on his dragon's smooth scales made Cato release tension he didn't know he was holding.

"I presume your journey was safe,"

"Ya, thanks for asking. Lordy was pleased to see me. I slew a few orky-s too,"

"Good. How goes the war?"

"Ya know. He needs more men, dragons, sword,"

"He knows I am trying?"

"Course that Lordy trusts ya,"

"What about the information I wanted?"

Cato felt Pendra's chest move as the dragon tried to clear her throat to speak *normally* in a whisper.

"Ya know. It wasn't the Lord Commander who send him here. It was ya father,"

"Why?"

"I don't know, Catty. Ya both gay?"

Cato smiled and shook his head.

"Why was he sent here in the first place?"

"He was about to be executed for treason and murder before ya father stopped it,"

Cato's eyes widened at the news. These were not light crimes against the Throne. Normally these criminals would have died in agony and in public for their crimes. But why didn't Caden? Why did his father stop it? Could Caden even be a threat to the trainees?

"He could be dangerous, Catty. He should go. Ya can't keep him,"

Cato stayed silent for a moment.

"Ya want me to get rid of him?"

"No, Pendra. If he is a traitor to the throne. And if my father sent him here for a reason. Then I will deal with him. No matter the outcome,"

GET YOUR FREE AND EXCLUSIVE SHORT STORY NOW! LEARN ABOUT NEMESIO'S PAST!

https://www.subscribepage.com/fireheart

About the author:

Connor Whiteley is the author of over 60 books in the sci-fi fantasy, nonfiction psychology and books for writer's genre and he is a Human Branding Speaker and Consultant.

He is a passionate warhammer 40,000 reader, psychology student and author.

Who narrates his own audiobooks and he hosts The Psychology World Podcast.

All whilst studying Psychology at the University of Kent, England.

Also, he was a former Explorer Scout where he gave a speech to the Maltese President in August 2018 and he attended Prince Charles' 70th Birthday Party at Buckingham Palace in May 2018.

Plus, he is a self-confessed coffee lover!

OTHER SHORT STORIES BY CONNOR WHITELEY

Blade of The Emperor
Arbiter's Truth
The Bloodied Rose
Asmodia's Wrath
Heart of A Killer
Emissary of Blood
Computation of Battle
Old One's Wrath
Puppets and Masters
Ship of Plague
Interrogation
Edge of Failure
One Way Choice
Acceptable Losses
Balance of Power
Good Idea At The Time
Escape Plan
Escape In The Hesitation
Inspiration In Need
Singing Warriors
Dragon Coins
Dragon Tea
Dragon Rider
Knowledge is Power
Killer of Polluters
Climate of Death
Sacrifice of the Soul
Heart of The Flesheater

Heart of The Regent
Heart of The Standing
Feline of The Lost
Heart of The Story
The Family Mailing Affair
Defining Criminality
The Martian Affair
A Cheating Affair
The Little Café Affair
Mountain of Death
Prisoner's Fight
Claws of Death
Bitter Air
Honey Hunt
Blade On A Train
City of Fire
Awaiting Death
Poison In The Candy Cane
Christmas Innocence
You Better Watch Out
Christmas Theft
Trouble In Christmas
Smell of The Lake
Problem In A Car
Theft, Past and Team

Other books by Connor Whiteley:

The Fireheart Fantasy Series
Heart of Fire
Heart of Lies
Heart of Prophecy
Heart of Bones
Heart of Fate

City of Assassins (Urban Fantasy)
City of Death
City of Marytrs
City of Pleasure
City of Pleasure

Agents of The Emperor
Return of The Ancient Ones
Vigilance
Angels of Fire

The Garro Series- Fantasy/Sci-fi
GARRO: GALAXY'S END
GARRO: RISE OF THE ORDER
GARRO: END TIMES
GARRO: SHORT STORIES
GARRO: COLLECTION
GARRO: HERESY
GARRO: FAITHLESS
GARRO: DESTROYER OF WORLDS
GARRO: COLLECTIONS BOOK 4-6

GARRO: MISTRESS OF BLOOD
GARRO: BEACON OF HOPE
GARRO: END OF DAYS

<u>Winter Series- Fantasy Trilogy Books</u>
WINTER'S COMING
WINTER'S HUNT
WINTER'S REVENGE
WINTER'S DISSENSION

<u>Miscellaneous:</u>
RETURN
FREEDOM
SALVATION

www.ingramcontent.com/pod-product-compliance
Lightning Source LLC
LaVergne TN
LVHW011901060526
838200LV00054B/4465